The Off-Beat Cinder Ella
who wants her shoe back...without the Prince.

by Anne Murray

illustrated by T.K. Diem Nguyen

Dedicated to Dr. Chris Moran,

who taught me to find my own magic

Not very long ago, a few streets over, lived a gal called Cinder Ella. That wasn't her real name, of course. Her mean stepsisters and the kids at school started taunting her with that name and it stuck. Like gum on a shoe bottom.

Her real name was Cheyenne.

But she hardly knew who she was any more. Her life had not been easy. Her beloved mother had died suddenly in a horrible car accident. Her father didn't mean to ignore her, but now he was responsible for earning a living and taking care of everything at home. Without any companionship.

Without any motherly guidance, Cinder Ella became an incorrigible tomboy. She invented all kinds of daring exploits. With her father distracted, she climbed trees straight to the top, rode horses without a saddle and took up archery without any instruction. Her clothing choices devolved into camo pants and high tops. And her dragon's tooth earrings. Her signature piece.

You could almost predict the next chapter in Cinder Ella's life. Her father, lonely and overworked, sought a new wife. That might have been o.k.—except that his new wife came with her own two daughters. Spoiled and bratty. Vain and extravagant. Useless. They definitely did not like moving into a new house and neighborhood. They made that very plain.

Speaking of plain, that was their favored term for Cinder Ella. They couldn't see past her clothes and cocky attitude. Not to mention those dratted dragon's tooth earrings. They had no interest in discovering her unique talents and big-hearted nature. No, they decided that, since she was younger and without anyone to stand up for her, that she would serve them. Night and day. Whenever they wanted. With whatever they wanted. Even pizza with Spam and brussels sprouts.

Of course, their mother endorsed this plan. It meant that she didn't have to worry about Cinder Ella and her feelings. Cinder Ella would be too busy to complain.

And busy she was. Cooking, cleaning, ironing, sweeping. Feeding the animals, which Cinder Ella loved. Scooping the animals' wastes, which she did not love. Soon her daily adventures became unending drudgery.

There didn't seem to be any end in sight.

No one even noticed Cinder Ella. Why would they? She was invisible, doing her daily chores. When she was in public, her ratty clothes and discouraged expression said, "Don't talk to me." Her downcast eyes said, "Don't notice me." Cinder Ella was sure that no one would be her friend. Certainly no guy would notice her.

Spending most of her time alone, Cinder Ella still had a few hijinks in her. One day she picked some blueberries. After making a thick syrup, she pasted some on strands of her hair, which turned purple. "Cool," she thought. It irritated her stepmother to no end. "Even cooler," she declared, satisfied.

Once in a while, making her stepsisters' beds, she would plant some marbles under their sheets. Or turn their bathroom towels inside out. Or sprinkle water on their homework so that it was smudged and untidy. (Not that they would have noticed.)

To celebrate Midsummer's Night, the high school Prom King decided to host a party-to-end-all-parties. Fancy dress, dancing to a live band and a midnight supper under the stars. A really big deal. Since he was considered royalty in their small town, his mother was hoping that he would find a suitable mate. She hadn't been pleased with the giggly, empty-headed girls that he had been bringing home. She wanted someone more sensible.

It was the Event of the Season. Well, actually, it was probably the event of the decade since most parties revolved around movie fests, pizza chowdowns or, heaven forbid, bowling. All the girls rushed out to buy their dream ball gowns until the shops were empty. Except for a pink-and-green polka-dotted dress in taffeta that even Cinder Ella would not wear.

She didn't have a dime to buy anything, anyway. Her stepmother wasn't planning to buy her an outfit, either. Plain as she was, her stepmother didn't want any competition for her two "lovely" girls.

So, on the night of the party, Cinder Ella made sure that her stepsisters' dresses were fitted properly as she wrestled them into their Spanx. Her older stepsister Melba had a splendid burgundy silk evening dress with off-the-shoulder style. Her younger stepsister Maude stuffed herself into a deep green velvet gown.

Cinder Ella ensured that their hair and make-up was immaculate. To accomplish this feat, Cinder Ella could have gotten a job as a stage make-up artist. Made them very pleasing to the eye. Too bad that the same could not be said for their sourpuss attitudes.

After they left in their brand-new baby blue Thunderbird, Cinder Ella sat down on the front steps by herself. Slowly the tears rolled down her face. Once again, she was overlooked. Left alone. She didn't care about the adored Prom King. His attentions didn't interest her. But, doggone it, what's a girl gotta do to have a little fun in this town?

Just as that thought settled, she closed her eyes and sighed. Would her life ever get better? Or would she always be smudged with cinders and eating the leftovers? Wasn't there any magic for her?

A small tap on her shoulder was ignored. Now what does anyone want with her? "Good grief, can't I just sniffle by myself?" A second tap. A croaky voice assaulted her ears. "Hey, girlie, I haven't got all day. Do you want my help or not?"

11

Help? Someone wanted to help her? She opened her eyes to the strangest sight--an older woman with a purple hat askew on her head, miles of floral fabric draped around her and a cane with a brass owl on its head. What the heck?

"Well, I can't say that I've enjoyed the assignment, but I've been ordered to keep watch over you. So far, you're not making great strides toward anything but more of the same. So I thought that a little direct intervention might be in order," she squeaked. "How about it? Are you up for that hoity-toity party?"

"In this?" Cinder Ella gasped, holding out her three-seasons-old flannel shirt. Her hair was sticking out all over her head from rushing around to help her stepsisters get ready for the party. Her mascara was running down her cheeks from her tears.

"Oh, bother, that's nothing," said her unexpected fairy godmother, tripping over her support shoes. "I can fix that in a flash."

"Well, let's do it, then," Cinder Ella agreed. "I could use a bit of fun."

O.K., but you can't expect me to do it all on my own," the old lady complained. "My arthritis has been kicking up and I can't lift any more."

"What do you need?" Cinder Ella asked expectantly.

"Bring me a pumpkin from the garden, one squirrel from the back yard and that little mouse hiding under the porch." When Cinder Ella brought the requested supplies, the slightly disorganized fairy lit a match to the end of her cane—well, she tried to, anyway. It took three tries before she managed to light the cane. (No one claimed that she was the most advanced fairy in the arsenal.) She waved the wand in an unsteady arc and muttered some words in a language that Cinder Ella didn't understand.

"Abracadiddlelifiddles—ahchoo! snort!—ah, just do it!"

14

Poof! All of a sudden, the pumpkin transformed into a candy-apple red Porsche 911. "Okaaay, now," thought Cinder Ella. The squirrel, now a handsome young man in a tux, opened the door in his role as her valet. And the mouse, with his hair in a ponytail, attired in a white shirt and red vest, set up a chair to style her hair.

With her hair on her head in a flattering style and her make-up repaired, the fairy godmother gave her new clothing. Instead of a traditional ball gown, which really didn't fit her personality, she was standing in an off-the-shoulder dress in beautiful flannel fabric with glitter. You see, it was easier for her fairy godmother to work with the fabric that she already had than to start from scratch. And her fairy godmother was diligent about saving effort and energy. Especially her own. Cinder Ella's dragon's tooth earring had been upgraded into fine precious metals with a pearl tooth. And on her feet? Clear plastic New Balance athletic shoes with a swirl on the toes. Perfect!

"O.K., girlie, you're ready to go. Go to the party and have fun! But realize that this is only a temporary fix. It will all dissolve at midnight, so make sure that you're out of sight by then. The rest is up to you."

With a flash that worked much better than the lighting of the cane, the arthritic fairy godmother was gone.

Cinder Ella drove her Porsche to the party. She mounted the expansive steps of the mansion and entered. The party was in full swing by then, but the guests gasped and parted for her entrance. She was stunning. No one recognized her in finery. No one recognized her with her hair done and eyes shining. But, most of all, no one recognized her with her confident stride and head held high.

"Who is this?" they whispered.

Always interested in a challenge, the Prom King himself walked over to her. "Will you dance with me?" He was so enthralled with her appearance and charming nature that he wanted to be with her all night at the party. How could he capture her attention?

But Cinder Ella didn't want to be dominated by one guy. Stretching her toes in freedom—remember those jazzy athletic shoes?—she wanted to meet more people. Walk out on the veranda. Have a snack.

So she ditched the Prom King after an obligatory dance or two. Wandered out to get a sniff of the night air. There she spotted a shy young guy who was scuffing his shoes and avoiding the crowd. "Hi there!"

The first thing that he noticed was her strange choice of footwear. "You look like you're more ready to take a hike than attend a dance party," he observed. "Well, I'd probably prefer it," she agreed.

"So what's your name?" he inquired.

"Cheyenne," she replied without a moment's hesitation.

"I'm David."

They walked around the grounds and enjoyed each other's company. Cheyenne decided to re-enter the party and grab some lemonade for them. As she was walking back with her drinks, she noticed the huge clock on the wall. About to strike midnight. Eeek!

She set the glasses down on the massive steps and ran. Time to disappear before her clothing did. As she pelted off, one of her shoelaces came undone and she lost her left New Balance shoe. No matter. Had to make tracks.

At the end of the party, both David and the Prom King were looking for her. Nowhere to be found.

"What happened?" said the Prom King. "She was captivating. I MUST find her."

He was flabbergasted to discover her abandoned athletic shoe on the steps. "Hah! She'll need this back. I'll find whoever fits this shoe."

As the gals left the party, the Prom King approached each one of them, holding the shoe and asking if it belonged to any of them. Most of them stuck their noses in the air and acted huffy that he would even suggest such a thing. "Wear that piece of garbage? Surely you're kidding."

So the Prom King had no luck.

He decided to put the shoe into his backpack and keep his eyes open for the likely owner. How hard could that be?

In the meantime, David wondered where Cheyenne had gone. He kept his ears and eyes open, looking for clues. One day he saw a gal in the distance, working hard around the house and whistling. He knew that the average gal didn't whistle. Too undignified. Could this be...?

When David found her with a bundle of hay on her pitchfork, Cheyenne was happy to see him. He offered to help and she was glad to have an extra pair of hands to finish her work. For once, she was able to finish before dark, so they sat on the steps and talked as though they were old friends.

After several weeks, the Prom King happened to walk by as Cinder Ella was chopping wood in the side yard. David, who had become her friend, was hauling a wheelbarrow full of debris to the trash pile. They were both hot and sweaty and laughing together as they worked. They had discovered that they had many things in common, including not liking crowds or bowling or pizza with weird ingredients. Better yet, David thought that her dragon's tooth earrings were groovy.

"Hey, are you the gal who belongs to this shoe?" said the Prom King.

"Well, first of all, I don't "belong" to any shoe," countered Cinder Ella.

"But does it fit your foot?" he wondered.

"Yes, I'm a 6 ½ medium, so it should fit. Who cares?"

"I do. I wanted to find that interesting and unusual woman who crashed my party. No one else caught my attention. I wanted to ask her if she would be my girlfriend."

"Really," replied Cinder Ella. 'You think that you're quite a Prince, don't you?"

The Prom King shuffled his feet and looked down. "Well, most girls would be flattered if I asked them."

"Well, go find one of them," she suggested."My friend David and I are having fun by ourselves. He's a mechanic and I want to learn accounting. I'm teaching him archery and he's going to teach me how to weld."

"So I don't need any Prom King, thank you."

Remember that your Prince can appear in any shape or size. He can have a degree or a title or a simple job. He can be perfectly groomed or have hair that stands up. What's important is that you laugh and play and feel at home with him. That's the magic.

If you enjoyed this book—or even if you didn't—would you do me the favor of leaving me a review?

It would be greatly appreciated.

If you liked this book, you might want to check out Peter Pants and Hammy & Gert.

Made in the USA
Columbia, SC
03 April 2020